This book belongs to:

_____

For Joel, and our favourite blue book of folk-tales – F.S.

To Rosie – K.L.

This paperback edition first published in 2021 by Andersen Press Ltd.

First published in Great Britain in 2020 by Andersen Press Ltd.,

20 Vauxhall Bridge Road, London, SW1V 2SA, UK

Vijverlaan 48, 3062 HL Rotterdam, Nederland

Printed and bound in China.

1 3 5 7 9 10 8 6 4 2

British Library Cataloguing in Publication Data available.

ISBN 978 1 78344 864 7

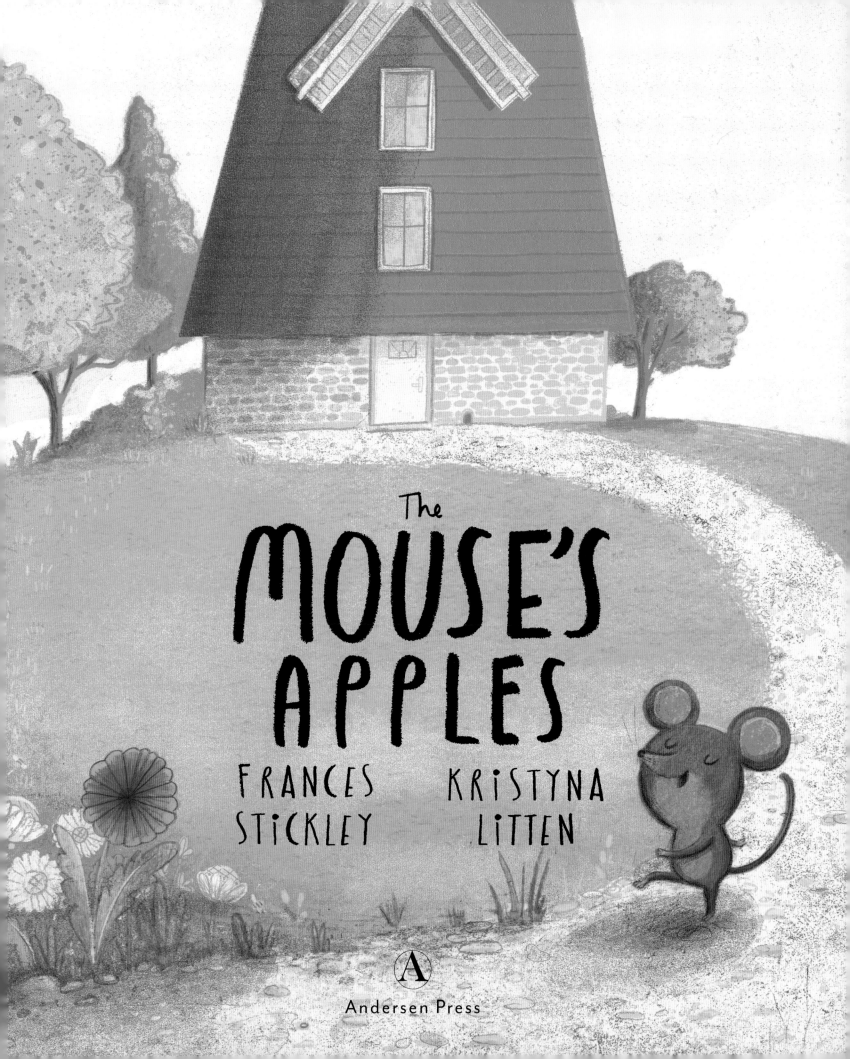

The MOUSE'S APPLES

FRANCES STICKLEY

KRISTYNA LITTEN

Andersen Press

A hungry mouse went walking
from her mousehole in the mill.
She dreamed of juicy apples as
she scampered down the hill.

Her tummy rolled
and rumbled

as she searched
along the floor.

So, imagine her
surprise to find not
one apple, but four!

The first was
red and rosy,
tucked inside
a flower
bed.

The next was pink and,

PLOP!

It almost fell
on to her head!

The third was
speckled yellow.

She dragged it
from the mud.

SQUELCH

The fourth was green
and gleaming

in the stream
within the
woods.

"Well," said Mouse, delighted.
"This must be my lucky day!"
She lined them up excitedly
and rolled them on her way.

"Four delicious apples!
That's the most I've ever found!"
But as she opened wide...

she heard a terrifying sound.

It grizzled and it grumbled,
then the voice said,

"STOP
RIGHT
THERE."

Mouse began to tremble
in the shadow of...

THE BEAR!

"Apples," boomed the bear,
"are my favourite tasty treat.
And I've been here all winter
without anything to eat."

Mouse's whiskers shivered as
she gazed up at the bear,
and nervously, she quivered,
"Well, they're mine, but we
could... share?"

"SHARE?"
said Bear.

"NO. I DON'T SHARE."

"That isn't fair!"
Mouse said.
"Fair?" said Bear.
"Oh, I don't care."

Mouse sighed and shook her head.

"Okay," Mouse sighed.
"You take them." But as she
walked away, she had a
clever thought and knew
exactly what to say.

"Bear," she said so sweetly,
"do you have to take them all?
I could have the fifth one
as it's only very small.

It's gone a little bad,"
she said. "It's turned
a little brown."
Bear seemed quite
befuddled as he stared
down at the ground.

"Five?" the bear said, puzzled.
"But I only counted four!"
Bear looked quite excited at the
thought there might be more.

"Please," said Mouse. "I'm hungry,
and it's old and brown and small."
"No," said Bear. "I do not care.
They're mine. I want them all!

Maybe, if you're lucky, then I'll let
you have the pips." And Bear
began to count them as he
laughed and licked his lips.

But as the bear was counting,
Mouse found a little leaf.

She rolled into a small
brown ball and gripped it
in her teeth and Bear
was so distracted as he muttered,
"Mine all mine!" that he didn't see the little mouse
had rolled into the line. Bear counted out the apples:

"ONE... TWO... THREE... and, FOUR..."

But wait – an extra apple. Mouse was right. There *was* one more! "It does look rather strange," he said. "It must be past its best."

But he popped it in his basket, just like the mouse had guessed.

Tucked inside the basket, Mouse barely even blinked for she knew that, if he found her, she'd be eaten in a wink.

Bear dreamed of juicy apples
as he walked out of the woods.

His tummy growled and grumbled
as he squelched across the mud.

He ambled through the orchard
humming ditties in his head,

so he didn't hear the
nibbles as he passed
the flower bed.

Bear opened up the basket
and he rushed inside his house,
but where there once were
apples, was a fat and happy...

Mouse!

Bear was flabbergasted.

"You tricked me! That's not fair!"

"Fair?" said Mouse, "but *you're* the naughty bear who doesn't share! And that's an awful shame," she sighed, "because, you see, I do."

"Here," said Mouse, and smiled.
"Look! I saved this one for you."
"For me?" said Bear, bewildered.
"But... I wasn't very fair."
He handed Mouse the apple.
"No, you found it fair
and square."

Then all at once, Bear realised
how good it felt to share.
"You know," said Mouse, "it's not
too late to be a better bear."
"It's not?" Bear asked. "It's not!" he
gasped. "Then now's the time to start."
And Bear seemed quite dumbfounded
by his sudden change of heart.
He said, "Could you forgive me?"
with a sorry, sideways glance.
"Of course," Mouse answered.
"Everyone deserves a
second chance."

Bear grinned from furry ear to ear.
"Oh, thank you, Mouse," he sighed.
"Friends?" he whispered, hopefully.
"Friends!" the mouse replied.